Lindsay
the Luck Fairy

Special thanks to Kristin Earhart

To Sarah. I'm so lucky to have you as a friend.

ISBN 978-0-545-48492-3

12 11 10 9 8 7 6 5 4 3 2 1   13 14 15 16 17/0

Printed in the U.S.A.   40

First printing, January 2013

Lindsay
the Luck Fairy

by Daisy Meadows

SCHOLASTIC INC.

The Fairyland Palace

Castle

Beach

Inn

Jack Frost's Ice Castle

Toberton

Hotel

Town Green

Wishing Well

Town Hall

Nature Preserve

Around the fairies, my magic cowers.
I seem weak against their powers.
When I battle them I sometimes get stuck,
But I'm just a guy with lots of bad luck.

The goblins are about to change my ways.
They'll bring an end to my unlucky days.
They'll steal a coin, a shamrock, and a hat.
Then I'll be lucky — imagine that!

With Lindsay the Luck Fairy's lucky pieces,
My magic power only increases.
My chilling spells will be so strong,
I'll take over Fairyland before too long!

**Find the hidden letters in the clovers
throughout this book. Unscramble all 8 letters
to spell a special lucky word!**

Hat Trick

Contents

Trip to Toberton

"I'm so glad you could come with us," Rachel Walker said to her best friend, Kirsty Tate. "I always have more fun when we're together."

"Me, too," Kirsty said. She grabbed Rachel's hand in the backseat of the car and smiled. The girls always shared such amazing adventures!

This time, they were headed to Toberton, a small village several hours from Rachel's house. Mrs. Walker was going to a convention at the Toberton Hotel over the weekend for work, and everyone else was coming along to enjoy the country air.

"You'll find a lot to do around Toberton, girls," Mrs. Walker said from the front seat. "When I was little, I stayed in a cottage there with my family. It's beautiful."

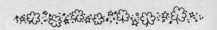

"That's not what you said when you first read the invitation to the convention. You said Toberton was spooky!" Mr. Walker remarked with a laugh.

"That's not exactly true," Mrs. Walker corrected him, smiling. She turned and looked into the backseat. "My brothers, who were much older, told me the woods were haunted with fairies, goblins, and leprechauns. I was so young that I believed them. I even imagined seeing green shadows hiding in the trees. It's silly, I know."

Rachel and Kirsty didn't think it sounded silly at all! The two girls *knew* that fairies and other magical creatures were real. In fact, they were friends with the fairies! The girls had assisted the fairies on many occasions. Whenever Jack Frost and his naughty goblins had evil plans, the king and queen of Fairyland asked Rachel and Kirsty for help.

"While Mom is in her meetings, we can explore the town and the nearby landmarks," Mr. Walker said from the driver's seat. "I'll bet there are some great wildflowers in the woods, too."

Kirsty and Rachel smiled at each other. Mr. Walker really liked flowers and wildlife.

"Don't forget that I have tomorrow afternoon off," Mrs. Walker added. "And if everything goes as planned with my speech, I can join you for the festival on Sunday."

Today was only Friday, but Sunday was St. Patrick's Day, and there would be a festival in the center of town to celebrate. The girls couldn't wait!

"It sounds like we'll be busy," Kirsty said, grinning with excitement.

"How long until we get there?" Rachel asked.

"Well, we would be there already, if we hadn't had to turn around," said Mrs. Walker.

"Don't worry, dear. We should still make it on time," Mr. Walker said.

Rachel bit her lip. Her mom had lost her glasses, and they'd had to go back home to get her other pair. Then they

had run into a
lot of traffic.
Now they were
running really
late. What
bad luck!

As soon as
they pulled
into the
hotel's circular
driveway, Mrs. Walker jumped out of
the car and rushed inside. Mr. Walker
opened the trunk and handed each girl
her own duffel bag. Then he grabbed the
bag that he and Mrs. Walker shared. As
he slammed the trunk closed, Rachel
thought she saw something flash by in a
shimmery glow.

"Did you see that?" Rachel whispered to Kirsty.

Kirsty looked around and shook her head. "No," she answered.

Rachel frowned. "It was probably nothing."

They walked into the hotel lobby, which had high ceilings and deep red curtains and carpets. "I'm excited to stay here. It's so fancy," Kirsty said, looking around with wide eyes.

"Yeah, but look at those dirty footprints," Rachel said, giggling. There was a muddy trail right in front of the check-in desk.

Before Kirsty could say anything, Mrs. Walker approached them. "Sorry, girls. The hotel lost our reservation,

and there aren't any open rooms here," she said with a frown.

"We'll have to go to the inn across town," Mr. Walker added. Rachel thought for a minute. "But the conference is here." "I know. It's very unlucky," Mrs. Walker agreed.

They all took their bags back out to the car. As Mr. Walker opened the

trunk, Rachel saw the same shimmer
again.

Kirsty grabbed Rachel's hand. "I saw
it, too," she whispered, pulling her friend
to the side. "Rachel, I think it was a
fairy!"

Something Shiny

"Oh, I hope it *is* a fairy!" Rachel said. "But where did she go?"

"I'm not sure," Kirsty said in a hushed voice. "We have to find her."

"Girls, I'm going to head into a meeting. You can take the bags to the inn with Dad," Mrs. Walker suggested, waving and going into the hotel.

"All right. Let's go!" Rachel's dad called.

Kirsty gave Rachel a meaningful look.

"Dad, could we walk over to the inn? I need to stretch my legs," Rachel said. "We were in the car forever!"

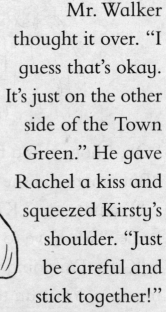

Mr. Walker thought it over. "I guess that's okay. It's just on the other side of the Town Green." He gave Rachel a kiss and squeezed Kirsty's shoulder. "Just be careful and stick together!"

As soon as he had given them the address and pulled out of the driveway,

Rachel and Kirsty started searching for a fairy. "Hello?" Kirsty whispered.

"Down here," a sweet, tinkling voice rang out.

Rachel scanned the ground until she saw a tiny fairy hidden in the spotted green ferns planted in front of the hotel. It was hard to see her because she was wearing a white and bright green dress that blended into the plants! "Hello,"

Rachel said, bending down. "I'm Rachel, and this is Kirsty."

"Oh, I'm so glad!" the fairy exclaimed. Her bright green eyes were filled with relief. "I was trying to find you, but I was chased by a bee and then I got locked in your trunk. It was all very unlucky. Finding you is the only lucky thing that's happened to me all day." She nervously twisted her red hair around her finger. "I'm not used to unlucky things happening. After all, I'm Lindsay the Luck Fairy!"

"It's nice to meet you, Lindsay," Kirsty

and Rachel said together. It was always fun to make a new fairy friend!

"It's wonderful to meet the two of you." Lindsay curtsied. "You're just who I was hoping to find. I need your help!"

"What's the matter?" Kirsty asked. "How can we help?"

"Jack Frost is causing trouble again," Lindsay explained. "This time, he sent his goblins to steal my three good-luck charms: a gold coin, a shamrock, and a black bowler hat with a green ribbon."

Rachel and Kirsty both frowned. Jack Frost again!

"My charms are in charge of luck, both in the fairy and the human worlds," Lindsay told them. "They make sure there is plenty of good luck to go around! The hat controls the luck of sports and games. The shamrock affects the luck of losing and finding things, and the gold coin is in charge of the luck that helps things go just as planned."

"Oh! Now I know why Mom lost her glasses," Rachel said. "That was very unlike her."

"And it explains why the hotel didn't save a room for us," Kirsty added.

"*And* why we ran into bad traffic that made us late," Rachel said. It didn't take the girls long to realize what a mess the world would be if they didn't help Lindsay!

"Jack Frost wants to control my charms himself. With all that luck, he could take over all the magic in Fairyland!" Lindsay buried her face in her hands.

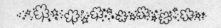

"Don't worry, Lindsay. We'll help you," Rachel assured her. "Do you have any idea where your charms are now?"

"I was outside watering my shamrock patch when I heard the goblins running away from my cottage. All at once, an icy blue blast of magic surrounded the goblins and they disappeared." Lindsay shook her head. "Then I heard an awful laugh. It was Jack Frost! He gave me a wicked smile and said, 'My goblins have your good-luck charms, my dear. You won't be able to find them in the human world. Without those charms, you'll have no luck at all!' before he disappeared. And he's right, I don't have good luck anymore — only bad luck!"

Rachel and Kirsty looked at each other sadly. Poor Lindsay!

Toberton Town Hall

"We'll help you," Kirsty told their new fairy friend. "Don't worry!"

Rachel nodded. "Do you think your good-luck charms are close by? Have you seen any goblins?" she asked.

"I can feel that the charms are close, but I haven't seen a single goblin," Lindsay answered, shrugging and looking

glum. "I don't even know where to start looking."

"Well, let's explore the town and let the magic come to us," Kirsty suggested. It was the same advice that the fairy queen had given the girls on their first fairy adventure, and it had always worked!

Lindsay tucked herself into the roomy pocket of Kirsty's wool jacket, and the three friends headed off.

The Toberton Town Green was a beautiful park in the middle of the town. There were playgrounds and ball fields as well as large, grassy areas for picnics. A small gazebo, a wishing well, and a wooded area dotted the far end of the green. It seemed like it was usually a lovely, peaceful place —

but not today. Today, the park was full of kids, and they were all arguing.

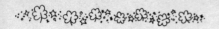

"Hey, that's not fair!" a kid with a basketball yelled.

"It is too fair. You're just unlucky," a boy wearing high-top sneakers said, snatching the ball away.

"You cheated!" a little girl playing hopscotch nearby cried.

"It's not my fault your stone landed there," another girl said, hands on her hips. "You have bad luck."

At once, Kirsty and Rachel knew what
the problem was. Lindsay's magic hat
was missing! It was in charge of making
sure there was plenty of good luck in
games and sports. "It sounds like lots of
people are having bad luck," Rachel said
thoughtfully.

"And no one is being a good sport,"
Kirsty agreed. "We need to find the
magic hat before things get any worse."

Looking around, they noticed a tall,
old building on the corner of the green.
"Look, it's the
Toberton Town
Hall," Kirsty
said, pointing.
"Maybe we
should go in
there. We

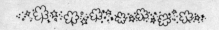

might get some ideas for where to look, since there's sure to be information about the town inside."

Rachel agreed, and they headed up the cobblestone walk.

"Girls, girls!" It was Lindsay, calling from Kirsty's pocket.

Kirsty carefully pulled open her pocket. "What is it, Lindsay?" she asked. Was something wrong?

"Did you hear those footsteps? It sounded like someone ran right past us," the little fairy explained.

Rachel and Kirsty shook their heads.

"We didn't see anything," Rachel said.

"Or hear anything," Kirsty added.

"*Hmm*, that's strange," Lindsay said. "Well, keep your eyes — and ears — open. Just in case."

"We will," Kirsty and Rachel reassured her as they walked into the hall. The inside of the building looked very old. The walls were made of large stones, and the only light came streaming through colorful stained-glass windows. There was a big room with an arched ceiling straight ahead of them. It was filled with long wooden benches and a podium.

"This must be where they have the town meetings," Rachel said. "A lot of people could fit in here."

"But it's empty now," Kirsty added, looking around. "Hello! Is anyone here?" she called out. Her words echoed back from the high ceiling.

"If there isn't anyone here, then I'm coming out for some fresh air." Lindsay flew out of Kirsty's pocket, soared up in a fancy figure eight, and landed on a large green-tinted statue.

"Hey, look at that," Rachel said. "It looks like a statue of a leprechaun."

"It is," Kirsty confirmed, reading from a plaque. "His name's Toby. He's Toberton's town leprechaun."

"Is he wearing a bowler hat, Lindsay?" Rachel asked. The statue had on a classic hat with a brim that curled up. A wide

ribbon wrapped
around the base of
the hat.

"Yes, he is! It
looks just like my
good-luck charm."
Lindsay sighed.
Suddenly, she

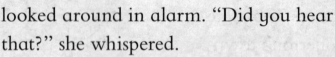

looked around in alarm. "Did you hear
that?" she whispered.

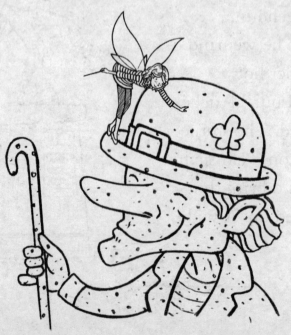

"No," Rachel admitted.

"It sounded like someone laughing," Lindsay said, fluttering to land on Rachel's shoulder. "I'm sure of it. And that someone is very close."

The girls looked at each other. Was Lindsay hearing things?

A Path
of Prints

"We believe you, Lindsay," Rachel said.
"But I wonder why you can hear the
laughter and we can't?"

"I don't know," Lindsay said, peering
around in confusion.

"Well, let's search. Maybe we can
figure out where the laugh came from,"
Kirsty suggested. She knew that they

were all thinking it might be a goblin. Those horrible goblins were cackling all the time!

They started searching the main room. As the friends looked around, the girls found some brochures for things to do in Toberton. They picked up a few to share with Rachel's parents. Then the three friends split up to look in the hallways and the smaller rooms of the town hall.

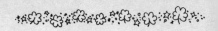

"Rachel, Lindsay! Come quick! I found something," Kirsty called.

Rachel came running. She found Kirsty bent down, looking at something close to the front door.

"Footprints!" Rachel gasped. "Just like the ones at the hotel."

"Maybe they belong to a goblin," Lindsay thought out loud. "And maybe that goblin has my lucky hat! Let's hurry!"

They followed the muddy path out the door and ran along the sidewalk, looking ahead to see if they could find whoever made the muddy footprints. Then, all at once, the footprints stopped.

"That's funny," Kirsty
said. "The path ends
right here. It's almost
like magic."

The three friends
scanned the sidewalks
and the town green.
They didn't see anyone
who could have made
the footprints, but
they did see a lot of
disappointed kids. The
kids were having very
bad luck playing their
games and sports.

"I feel so bad for them," Lindsay said,
covering her eyes with her hands. "I
can't even watch. It makes me too sad."

"Then you
should watch that
team over there,"
Rachel said,
pointing. "They

have great soccer skills, and they seem to have good luck, too." Rachel admired the players for a minute before realizing something. "Hold on . . ."

"They *are* good," Kirsty said.

"And they're goblins!" Rachel added.

The team was all wearing warm-up suits with the hoods up over their heads. Extra-large sneakers covered their big feet, but

their green hands and noses stuck out
and gave them away.

"If they're
playing that
well, then
they *must*
have my
lucky hat,"
Lindsay
decided.
The three
friends
watched the
soccer game
closely. A girl from the other
team made a great soaring kick.
The ball headed straight for the goal. But
at the last moment, the ball seemed to

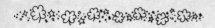

swerve around the goal and land just
outside the net. What horrible luck!
When the goalie ran over to grab the
ball, he cackled.

"He's a goblin, too," Kirsty said.

"And he's wearing my lucky hat under
his hood!" Lindsay cried.

"We have to get it!" Rachel declared,
taking off across the green at full speed.

As she ran down
the hill, she
stumbled into
a somersault.
She began to
roll faster
and faster until
she was out of
control!

Rachel rolled
to a dizzy stop at the bottom of the hill.
Lindsay and Kirsty hurried to catch up
with her, but Kirsty tripped on her
shoelace and landed right on top of
Rachel.

"Ouch." Kirsty groaned. "Are you
okay, Rachel?"

"I think so," Rachel answered.

"I'm sorry, girls. That's more bad luck,"
Lindsay said as her friends stood up.

Kirsty sighed. "And we aren't even
playing a game."

"Oh, yes you are," a gruff voice came
from the nearby soccer field. It was a
goblin, the tall one wearing Lindsay's

special hat. "The game is called Keep Away, and we're keeping the hat away from you. You're so unlucky, you'll never get it!"

Unlucky
Keep Away

All the goblins in warm-up suits
laughed. The tall goblin took the lucky
hat off his head and threw it straight
into the air. Kirsty gasped as she tried
to figure out where it would land. The
hat swirled around — and then
magically zoomed right into another
goblin's hands!

45

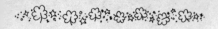

"Come and get it," the goblin cried. He waved the black hat over his head and ran into the woods. The rest of the goblins scrambled off behind him.

"Hey, that's not fair!" Kirsty cried. "We weren't ready."

"Ready or not, this might be our only chance." Lindsay flew off in hot pursuit of the goblins.

Rachel and Kirsty started to chase them, too, but soon, Kirsty had to stop. "Go ahead," she yelled to Rachel. "I have to tie my shoes *again*." Kirsty guessed that this was more bad luck.

Rachel glanced back at her friend, and then ran smack into a giant tree trunk. *Ouch!* "Really bad luck," she mumbled. Stunned, she took a deep breath, shook her head, and began running again.

Kirsty soon caught up, and the girls followed the goblins' nasty laughter.

"There's a stream ahead," Rachel pointed out. "Let's jump it." She ran ahead and leaped right over the brook. Kirsty prepared herself for the jump, but tripped on her takeoff. She landed in the muddiest part of the stream and splashed murky water all over Rachel. "We're drenched!" she cried.

"We have to keep going. The goblins are just up ahead," Rachel insisted.

Before long, the girls came to a clearing and ducked behind a tree, so they wouldn't be seen. The goblins were running around, tossing the lucky hat back and forth. They caught it easily every time.

One goblin was even doing somersaults between his throws. "I'm the best. Watch this!" he yelled. He threw the hat up

high and did a cartwheel before it came
back down.

Just then,
Lindsay
flew up to
the girls.
She landed
on Kirsty's
shoulder,
looking
sad. "I have
never felt so
unlucky," she
said. "They'll
never drop the hat."

"Oh, yes they will," Kirsty said.
"That goblin is extra lucky because
the hat and its magic are close to him.

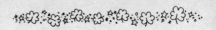

"That's right," Lindsay answered.

"Then I have a plan." Kirsty whispered her idea to Rachel and Lindsay. "I think it could work," Lindsay agreed, looking hopeful and fluttering her wings.

Lindsay quickly turned Rachel into a fairy, and Kirsty waited until her two friends had flown high into the sky

together. Then she approached the
bragging goblin.

"You're very good at that," she said to
him with a big smile.

"Oh, yes I am," the goblin agreed.
"I'm the best."

Kirsty pretended to think hard. "I
wonder if you're good enough to do a
somersault and two cartwheels before

the hat
comes back
down." She
raised an
eyebrow
at the
goblin.

"I'm sure
I am," the
goblin
boasted.

"You'd have to throw your hat very
high," she said.

The other goblins all agreed that their
friend could do it.

"I'd love to see it," Kirsty said, looking
up to make sure that Rachel and Lindsay
were still flying overhead.

"Just watch," the goblin huffed.
"Ready?" He threw the hat high in the
air. The goblins all cheered as their
friend did a somersault and then spun
into two perfect cartwheels.

While the goblins
watched, Rachel
and Lindsay
swooped down
and grabbed
the lucky bowler
hat from the
air. Lindsay
instantly shrunk it to its Fairyland size
and placed it on her head. "Hooray!"
she cheered, and gave Rachel a big
hug. "Tell Kirsty thank you for me. I
want to get the hat back to Fairyland
right away."

Down below, the goblins were waiting
for the hat to return.

"What happened?" asked the goblin
who had just finished cartwheeling.
"Where'd it go?"

"You threw it too high," the other
goblins complained. "Why did you have
to show off?"

As the goblins were busy arguing,
Kirsty snuck away. She met Rachel in

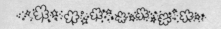

the woods. Lindsay had already changed her friend back to her human size. They gave each other high fives.

"We found the first lucky charm," Rachel said. "Now we just have two more to go."

"And we have two more days," Kirsty said with a smile. "I have a feeling our luck is starting to change!"

Lost and
Found Luck

Contents

A Classic Castle

"Here we are. We finally made it!" Mr. Walker announced. He pulled the car into a small gravel parking lot. "I wasn't sure we'd ever get here."

"Yes. We were a mess, but we're here now," Mrs. Walker said. She sounded relieved.

Rachel Walker smiled across the

backseat at her best friend, Kirsty Tate. They knew exactly why they were running late. They had all misplaced something that morning. Then they got lost on their drive to the castle. But Rachel and Kirsty knew there was a good reason for that!

"I'm glad you have the day off, Mom," Rachel said, unbuckling her seatbelt.

"We'll all have a lot of fun," Kirsty agreed. "I'm especially looking forward  to the picnic." Mr. and Mrs. Walker had packed sandwiches and sweets for their trip. Kirsty and Rachel could hardly wait for the brownies at the bottom of the picnic basket! At that moment, only one thing excited them more than those yummy brownies — fairies!

Rachel and Kirsty were in the middle of another fairy adventure. They had already found one of Lindsay the Luck Fairy's good-luck charms. Now there was good luck in games and sports again! But Lindsay needed more help. Her other two charms were still missing. One of them, the shamrock, controlled the luck of finding (and losing) things. Since the shamrock was gone, now people were losing things all of the time. It was why they couldn't find

the castle that morning. They had
lost their way! Things really were a
mess. Kirsty and Rachel hoped they
would find one of Lindsay's
charms today.

"I'm excited to be
here, too," Mrs.
Walker said as she
got out of the car.
"I think this is
the park where I
played with my
brothers and
cousins all those
years ago. I
remember the
castle and the woods.
And the windy beach."

Kirsty gasped when she saw the castle. It was built of old white stone, and it had a wooden drawbridge. A colorful flag flew above the tall bell tower. The castle looked like something out of a book. "I can't wait to explore in there. Can you?" Rachel asked her best friend. "It looks like a great hiding place for one of Lindsay's charms."

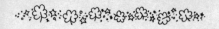

"But the castle is enormous. How will we ever track them down?" Kirsty wondered.

"Maybe the magic will come to us," Rachel said.

Mr. Walker took a deep breath and smelled the salty seaside air. He walked over to Rachel's mom. "So this is where you got lost and saw a spooky green leprechaun when you were a kid, huh?" Rachel's dad said with a delighted laugh. "Was he spying on you?"

Mrs. Walker shook her head. "I'm not sure he was spying on me," she answered. "I think he was . . . oh, never mind. That was a long time ago." She pushed her dark hair behind her ear. "And we all know there wasn't a *real* leprechaun."

"Don't worry. I'll protect you," Mr. Walker said, putting his arm around his wife.

Rachel and Kirsty looked at each other. They knew Rachel's dad was just joking with her mom, but Mrs. Walker had sounded serious.

"Is it possible? Did your mom see a real leprechaun?" Kirsty whispered.

"I don't know.
It sounds
mysterious,"
Rachel said.
"We'll have
to be on the
lookout."

"On the
lookout?
For what?"
a tiny voice
asked.

The girls peered around. Lindsay the
Luck Fairy was fluttering right behind
them! "Oh, Lindsay! It's great to see
you," Rachel said. She lowered her
voice. "But we don't want anyone else
to spot you."

"You can hide in my backpack," Kirsty suggested. "As soon as Rachel's parents are gone, we'll tell you everything."

Wildflower Watch

"Remember, meet us on the beach in two hours," Mrs. Walker called.

"We won't forget," Rachel said, waving to her parents. "Have a good nature walk! Don't get lost," she joked, but immediately wished she hadn't. With the lucky shamrock missing, anything could happen!

Kirsty waved, too. "We don't have much time," she said to Rachel. While Rachel's parents looked for wildflowers, Kirsty and Rachel would be looking for Lindsay's missing magic charms.

Kirsty unzipped her backpack, and Lindsay flew out. "Any ideas where we should start?" Rachel asked their fairy friend. "*Hmm,*" Lindsay thought out loud. "One of the charms is close. I can feel it."

"It looks like we might be the only ones at the park so far," Kirsty said.

"I'll hide on Rachel's shoulder, just in case," Lindsay said.

Kirsty shivered as they walked across the drawbridge. The wind whipped through her hair.

They bought tickets from one of the guards just inside the castle walls. She gave them a map of the castle grounds that they could share.

Rachel unfolded the map. "The castle is really big," she said.

"Maybe we should start in the gardens," suggested Kirsty.

"Sounds good to me," whispered Lindsay. "And don't forget to look for goblins, too. If they're here, we'll know we're on the right track."

The girls walked across the stone courtyard and entered the colorful gardens. There were rows of yellow and red tulips, and patches of deep blue irises. Beyond all the flowers, there was a grassy lawn and a forest of tall trees.

"Let's walk all the way around the
lawn," Lindsay said.

"Okay." Kirsty and Rachel both
shrugged. It was going to be hard to find
something so small in a place so big.

"Can you do a spell that might give us
a hint?" Rachel asked the little fairy.
"Maybe it could tell us which direction
to go."

"Sadly, no," Lindsay said. "Jack Frost's magic is hiding the charms, and his magic is very strong. Oh, but I just thought of something. I could do a spell to make the charm glimmer! That will make it easier to see." Lindsay smiled, pleased with herself. But then her smile quickly disappeared.

"What's wrong?" Kirsty asked.

"I've lost my wand!" Lindsay said, looking around. She flew off Rachel's shoulder and began searching the ground. "I can't do any magic without my wand."

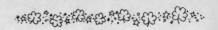

"When did you last have it?" Rachel asked.

Lindsay's eyes were wide. "I'm not sure. It must have slipped right out of my hand."

Rachel and Kirsty immediately dropped on their hands and knees and began to search. But a fairy wand was even smaller than a magic charm! At least the charms had grown larger when they entered the human world.

"Oh, it's no use. This is more of my horrible luck," Lindsay muttered. "Besides, it is more important to find the charms. I can get another wand back in Fairyland, but the shamrock and the gold coin are both one of a kind."

"Then let's go back to looking for them. Maybe we'll find your wand, too," Kirsty said.

Rachel didn't say anything. She had a funny feeling that someone was watching her. She turned around and saw a dark green shadow in the trees. "Kirsty, Lindsay . . . I think someone is watching us. In the trees. It might be a goblin."

Lindsay and Kirsty slowly glanced at the trees. The shadow seemed short, and

it looked like there
might be a hat on
its head.

"I see it, too,"
Kirsty whispered.
"It looks like
there's only one
of them."

"Maybe it isn't a goblin at all," Lindsay
said quietly. "Maybe it's a leprechaun!"

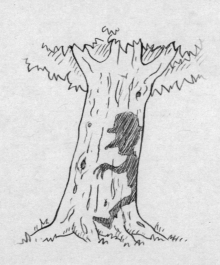

Double Chase

A leprechaun! Rachel and Kirsty stared at the figure in the shadows again.

"It looks like he's wearing a bowler hat, just like the statue in the town hall," Rachel said quietly. But they could only see the outline of the figure. They couldn't see his clothes or his face.

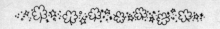

"We could follow him," Lindsay suggested.

"I thought all leprechauns were troublemakers," Kirsty said. "I heard that they steal people's luck."

"I heard that, too," Rachel agreed.

"That's probably just an old folk tale. There's no way *all* leprechauns are mischievous," Lindsay said. "Besides, I already lost all of my luck."

"Look! He's moving!" Rachel pointed into the woods.

The girls and Lindsay started to follow

the figure. They moved slowly at first, hoping he wouldn't notice.

"Hey, look!" a gruff voice yelled out. "There's someone in the woods!"

The girls turned around to see a group of boys running toward them. The boys were all dressed in jeans and striped shirts. They wore baseball caps that covered their faces.

"Get that guy!" another boy yelled.

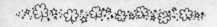

At once, Rachel and Kirsty realized
that the boys were chasing the shadow in
the woods. The next moment, the girls
realized the boys were . . . goblins!

"It's the guy in the black hat and funny
shoes," cried a third goblin. "The one
who stole our charms!"

"*Their* charms?" Rachel and Kirsty said in surprise.

"Those are *my* charms," Lindsay said, stomping her tiny foot on Rachel's shoulder.

"So, someone took the charms from the goblins," Kirsty said. "And the goblins think it was the person in the woods!"

"We have to catch him!" Rachel insisted. Rachel and Kirsty took off running into the woods. They crunched through last fall's leaves and ducked under low branches. Lindsay stayed perched on Rachel's shoulder and grabbed on to the collar of Rachel's jacket so she wouldn't fall. The girls ran after the goblins — and the shadow — for some time.

"I wish I had my wand," Lindsay said. "Then I could turn you into fairies. You could fly much faster."

It was true. The shadow was fast —
too fast to catch. The girls could see
him jump onto a log way up ahead.
He turned around and stuck his hands
out on either side of his head, but
they couldn't see his face. He was too
far away!

"I think he just
stuck his tongue
out at us," Kirsty
said between
breaths.

Rachel laughed.
"That's kind of
funny," she said.
The goblins
didn't find it funny at all. They
yelled and ran even harder.

"He's too far ahead," Kirsty said,
panting.

"Let's take a break," Rachel agreed.
When they came to a log, they stopped
and took a seat. Lindsay flew down to sit
on Rachel's knee.

"Well, at least we know that the goblins
don't have my charms," Lindsay said.

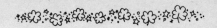

"Do you think the shadowy guy really has them? Does he even know what they are?" Kirsty wondered.

"I'm not sure," Lindsay said.

The girls and the fairy sat quietly, catching their breath.

A robin landed on the ground near them. It chirped, pecking at the grass.

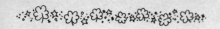

The bird looked up at Rachel, Kirsty, and Lindsay, chirping over and over.

"Hi, pretty bird," Kirsty said. The robin chirped and pecked again. "Hey, what's that?" Kirsty reached down and picked up a piece of paper near the robin's beak. She carefully unfolded it.

"There's writing on it!" Rachel said. "It looks like a poem."

"Or," Lindsay added thoughtfully, "a clue."

A Clever Clue

The paper was the size of a postcard. It
was stiff and yellow with age. Kirsty
held it in her hands so Rachel and
Lindsay could see.

"The writing looks fancy," Rachel
said, "and old."

"Lindsay, why do you think this paper
is a clue?" Kirsty asked.

"Didn't the leprechaun stop by this log?" the fairy answered. "Maybe he dropped it."

"Maybe it leads to one of the charms," Rachel said.

Kirsty nodded. "We don't know if he really is a leprechaun yet," she reminded her friends. "But let's see what the paper says." She began to read:

May the light of friendship guide you.
May the power of love keep your hearts true.
When the luck of the Irish seems to have
  left you,
May the chime of the bells give you hope
  anew.

"That's so pretty," Rachel said with
a sigh.

"I like it," Kirsty agreed. "But it doesn't
sound like a clue. It doesn't say anything
about a shamrock or a gold coin."

"It was worth a
try," Lindsay said.

"I'll hold on to it,
just in case," said
Kirsty, folding the
paper and sliding it
into her pocket.

Lindsay sighed. "I thought we had finally found some good luck. What should we do now?"

"Let's look at the map," Rachel suggested. "Maybe we can figure out where the goblins and the leprechaun went." Rachel reached for one back pocket, then the other. "Oh, no! I lost it."

"More bad luck," Lindsay said.

"We don't need the map," Kirsty said to her friends, trying to look on the bright side. "Let's just go back in the castle. We can listen for the goblins to return there, and then track them down."

"They might help lead us to the leprechaun," Rachel agreed.

Lindsay perched on Rachel's shoulder again, and the two girls walked into the castle courtyard. At once, they heard yells echo off the stone walls. "That must be the goblins," Kirsty said, excited.

"But they sound far away." Rachel paused. "I have an idea." She walked over to one of the guards on duty.

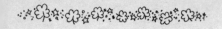

"Excuse me? We lost our group. Can you hear them? They might be calling for us."

"Yes, miss," the guard said. "They are quite loud. They must be down in the dungeon, from the sound of it."

"Oh, thank you!" Rachel said.

After the guard gave them directions, Rachel and Kirsty headed for

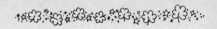

the dungeon. There was a wide, winding staircase that was lit by torches.

As the girls went down the steps, the goblins' yells grew louder. When they were almost to the bottom of the stairs, they heard footsteps. There was a flash in the shadows, and someone ran right past them.

The girls gasped. "Do you think that was the leprechaun?" Kirsty asked, surprised.

Just then, the band of goblins rushed by.

"It must have been," Rachel said. She started to follow them, but Kirsty caught her arm.

"Listen," Kirsty insisted.

"To what? I can only hear the goblins yelling," Rachel said, "and some chimes."

"Yes, chimes," Kirsty said excitedly. A sweet song carried through the air. It sounded like many bells tolling at the same time.

"Why does that ring a bell?" Lindsay wondered, ducking out from under Rachel's hair.

"I think the poem really was a clue!" Kirsty exclaimed. She reached for her back pocket, but didn't find anything there. "Oh, no! I lost the paper! Just my luck."

"I remember the last line," Lindsay said.

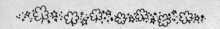

"'May the chime of the bells bring you hope anew.'"

"Yes! The chime of the bells — the bell tower!" Kirsty said.

"We have to go!" Rachel agreed. The girls spun around and began running up the stone steps, two at a time.

A Charming Poem

The song of the bells still rang in the air. "You really think the poem is a clue?" Rachel said between short breaths.

"I hope so!" Kirsty said. "We have to meet your parents soon, and we don't have any other ideas."

Lindsay was too excited to stay on Rachel's shoulder. She flew between the

girls as they raced up the steps of the bell
tower, her fingers crossed.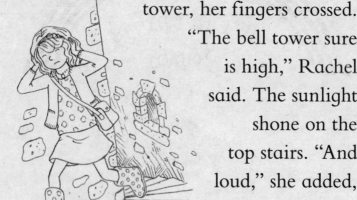
"The bell tower sure
is high," Rachel
said. The sunlight
shone on the
top stairs. "And
loud," she added,
covering her ears.
"That's why it's
such a great hiding place!" Kirsty said.

They stepped up onto the platform.
Four openings looked out on the garden,
the woods, the courtyard, and the ocean.
"Oh, it's beautiful!" Rachel said, looking
out at the waves crashing onto the
sandy beach.

"I agree," Lindsay said. Then she gasped

and pointed above them. "Look! My lucky shamrock charm is right up there!"

Kirsty and Rachel looked up to see the green charm. It was tied to the clapper of one of the giant brass bells with a glittery green ribbon. Like magic, the chiming of all the bells stopped at that moment.

"Hooray!"
Lindsay cried as
she flew up to
claim the
charm. She
hovered in the
air, tugging and
pulling on the
shamrock.

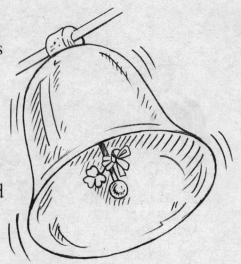

"There's just one problem," the fairy
grunted. "It's tied too tight. I can't get
it down."

That was a big problem. The bell
was far too high for Kirsty or Rachel to
reach.

"Without my wand, I can't do a
thing," Lindsay explained. She sighed
sadly. "I thought finding the shamrock

would
solve
my problems.
But my wand is
still lost."

Kirsty and Rachel looked at each other. What could they do?

"Maybe I have something in my backpack that would help," Kirsty said, but she wasn't all that hopeful. She knew she had taken out her art kit before she packed for the picnic. Rachel watched as her friend rummaged through the

pockets. At last, Kirsty came to the
pouch that held her extra sweater. It was
where Lindsay had hidden earlier.

"Oh! Lindsay, it's your wand!" Kirsty
cried with glee. She held the tiny wand
up in the air, gripped between her thumb
and finger.

"Oh, what luck!" Lindsay said, doing
a happy loop as she flew down to

Kirsty. The joyful fairy took the
wand and gave it a twirl, looking up
toward the bell. Immediately, the green
ribbon untied itself. The shamrock
charm floated down and landed in
Lindsay's arms. It shrunk down to its
Fairyland size.

"I hate
losing
things,"
Lindsay said
with a grin.
"Thanks so
much for helping
me find my
shamrock.
King Oberon
and Queen Titania will be very relieved.
Now fairies and people won't be unlucky
and lose things all the time."

"And, if they do," Rachel
added, "they'll have much better luck
finding them!"

The three friends laughed.

Rachel looked out of the bell tower
again. "Kirsty, I can see my parents!

They're heading down to the beach. We should hurry."

"And I should hurry back to Fairyland," said Lindsay. "I want to share the good news with everyone there, but I'll be back. We still have one more good-luck charm to find!"

At once, Lindsay's freckled face disappeared behind a rush of magic

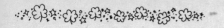

shamrock glitter. In a moment, the
whirlwind was gone — and so was
Lindsay.

"What a wonderful adventure," Kirsty
said as they began to walk down the
stairs. "A fun fairy friend, a poem that
was really a secret clue, and maybe even
a tricky leprechaun."

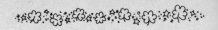

"And now we're headed for a picnic!" Rachel agreed.

"With brownies!" Kirsty remembered.

"I can't imagine a more magical day," Rachel said.

Kirsty smiled at her best friend. "Well, there's always tomorrow!"

Good as
Gold

Contents

A Morning Mix-up

The next morning, Rachel Walker and Kirsty Tate woke to the sound of running water just outside their window. They were staying at the Luck of the Irish Inn, and their room looked out on the Toberton Town Green. A clear brook wound its way through the green's woods and meadow.

"I'm glad my mom asked us to come with her. It's so nice here," said Rachel. While Mrs. Walker worked in the village, Mr. Walker and the girls were enjoying the countryside.

"And it's even nicer to be helping our fairy friends," Kirsty said. "But we only have one day left to find Lindsay's last lucky charm."

"That's right. Mom has her big speech today, so we leave this afternoon." Rachel frowned as she quickly got out of bed and pulled on some dark jeans and a striped sweater.

"I hope she gets done early. She can't miss the St. Patrick's Day festival on the town green," Kirsty said. Each year, the town of Toberton hosted a big festival to celebrate the holiday.

"It should be fun!" Rachel agreed. "I can't wait to see the decorations and play the games."

"But first we have to help Lindsay," said Kirsty.

"Actually, first we have to go to the park with my dad," Rachel reminded her friend. "He wants to go on a nature walk. He's looking for a special flower."

Kirsty laughed as she brushed her hair. "That's okay. We should let the magic come to us, anyway." The girls headed down to the inn's dining room where Mr. Walker was waiting. He was drinking coffee and looking at a book about wildflowers.

"Good morning, girls," he said with a smile. "Are you hungry?"

"Yes!" they replied. Kirsty could hear her belly rumble. She had been thinking about blueberry pancakes all morning.

"You need a big breakfast," Rachel's dad said. "I already ordered for you. I want to tell you about our big day while we wait. I have it all planned out!"

Rachel gulped when she heard her dad's words. That could be a problem. Lindsay's last missing charm was a gold coin. It was in charge of the special luck it took for everything to go just as planned. It also prevented things from going wrong at the last minute. Since Jack Frost's goblins stole the coin, nothing had been going right!

The server arrived and placed steaming bowls in front of each of the girls. Kirsty looked down. Lobster stew? For breakfast? Her stomach turned.

"Thank you," Rachel said to the server.

It was hard to hide her disappointment. She had wanted French toast, but she took the stew as a sign. They needed to find that gold coin. And fast!

Mr. Walker didn't notice that anything was wrong. "You should eat up. We need lots of energy if we're going to find the marsh pennywort," he declared.

After breakfast, Rachel pulled Kirsty aside. "I'm worried," she whispered.

"Think of all the other things that could go wrong. We have to find that coin!"

"I know," agreed Kirsty. "Lobster stew is horrible for breakfast. I'm afraid to see what he has planned for lunch!"

"We have to get back from the nature walk as fast as we can," Rachel said.

"But we still don't know where the coin is," Kirsty reminded her friend. "Maybe it's in the park."

"Good point," Rachel said. "Let's hope Lindsay shows up soon! She might know where to look."

Mr. Walker approached the girls. He had three bike helmets in his hands. "I

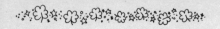

forgot that Mom took the car, but we can bike to the park."

"How long will it take to get there?" Rachel asked.

"Not long," Mr. Walker said.

They pulled on their backpacks, snapped on their helmets, and went outside. Rachel was relieved to see three bikes parked at the bike rack.

Mr. Walker looked at his watch. "The Wildflower Walk is at ten o'clock. If we get there early, I can talk to the guide before it starts."

They climbed on their bikes and headed off, but soon had to stop.

"The street is closed," Kirsty said, reading a sign.

"It must be because of the festival,"

Mr. Walker guessed. "We'll have to go
the other way."

Rachel sighed. Would *any* of their plans
work out? What would happen with her
mom's big speech? And where was
Lindsay? She looked over at Kirsty. She
could tell her friend was worried, too.

Mushroom Mania

After several wrong turns and long dusty roads, Mr. Walker and the girls finally made it. The park was beautiful! They could see a group of people up ahead.

"We're just in time," Mr. Walker said. "I'll hurry over and talk to the guide."

Rachel nodded. As she and Kirsty parked the bikes, they heard someone clap.

"Hello, everyone," said a man with sandy-brown hair and a beard. He was wearing a puffy orange vest. "My name is Logan, and I will be your guide."

Rachel looked over. They were too late! Mr. Walker didn't get to talk to the guide. More ruined

plans! "If you gather around," Logan went on, "we can start our Mushroom Walk."

Many people in the group groaned. "I thought this was the Bird Walk," a woman with binoculars said.

"I though it was the Rosebud Walk," another woman called out. She was looking at a brochure and shaking her head. "I'm sorry," Logan said. "There

have been a lot of misunderstandings lately, but today is the Mushroom Walk. It'll be fun."

Mr. Walker turned to Rachel and Kirsty. "I'm sorry, girls. Another change of plans, but let's stay anyway. I can still look for the pennywort while we walk."

Kirsty covered her mouth so that Mr. Walker wouldn't see her laugh. "He really does love nature," she said to Rachel.

"I do, too!" a tiny voice said.

At once, Rachel and Kirsty swung around. "Lindsay!" they whispered excitedly. The

fairy quickly tucked herself behind
Rachel's hair.

"Do you know where the gold coin
is?" Rachel asked. "Is
it close by?"

"Oh, girls," Lindsay
replied with a frown.
"I have no idea, but
we have to find it
soon. Nothing is
going right!"

"Please keep quiet," the guide called
from the front of the group. "We don't
want to scare the birds and animals."

"I don't think he was talking to us,"
Kirsty said quietly to Rachel and Lindsay.
"I think he was talking to those boys."

Rachel looked at the band of noisy
boys nearby. They were at the back of

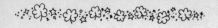

the group, kicking at the ground and
mumbling. All of the boys were wearing
green leprechaun suits, black
buckled shoes, and large
bowler hats that covered
their faces. Rachel
knew at once that
they weren't boys.

"They're
goblins!"
Lindsay
whispered.
"Maybe they
know where my
lucky coin is!"

Kirsty and Rachel
moved closer to the
goblins, hoping to hear
what they were saying.

"Why are we looking for just one gold coin?" a goblin with a flower in his hat said. "I want a million gold coins."

"But if we find the magic gold coin, all of Jack Frost's plans will come true," another goblin said. "Yeah, he'll be superpowerful and will rule Fairyland. The fairies can be his servants, and he'll finally stop bossing *us* around," a goblin with a long nose added.

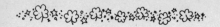

Rachel and Kirsty quickly stepped away.

"That's horrible!" Kirsty exclaimed.
"We can't let them find the gold coin."

"If they do, it will mean nothing but
bad luck for all of Fairyland," Lindsay
said solemnly. "I can't let that happen!"

"Don't worry, Lindsay," Rachel
comforted her. "We found your other
two good-luck charms. We'll find
the coin, too."

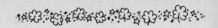

"We should stay close to the goblins," said Kirsty. "We can make sure they don't find it."

"That's a good plan," Lindsay said. Then all the friends frowned. With the coin missing, all their plans so far had turned into absolute messes. This one *had* to work!

Greedy Goblins

As Rachel and Kirsty followed the
group, they watched the goblins closely.
The goblins did not listen to the guide
at all, but the rest of the group was very
interested. Each time Logan brushed
leaves off a patch of mushrooms, they
gasped.

At one point, the goblins crowded around something. "What are they looking at?" Kirsty asked. Loud knocking sounds came from the goblin huddle.

"Excuse me," Logan called out. "Please stop playing with the donation box."

The goblins quickly stepped away, and the girls could see a clear box with a slot at the top attached to a wooden post. It was where people could give money to the park.

"The goblins were looking for the gold coin in the park's donation bin," Rachel said with a giggle. "They look embarrassed."

"They should!" Lindsay insisted. "That money isn't theirs. Neither is the lucky coin."

The group made their way through the
woods, making stops here and there.
The girls stayed close to the goblins the
whole time.

All at once, one of the goblins stopped.
"What was that?" he asked, looking
nervous. "I saw something behind
that tree."

"Was it that pesky green guy again?" the goblin with the long nose asked. "*We're* green guys!" said another goblin, putting his hands on his hips.

"No, I mean the one that tricked us and stole the charms," said the long-nosed goblin. "I hope it wasn't him. He gives me the creeps!"

Rachel and Kirsty looked at each other. Was the leprechaun in the woods? Did he have the gold coin?

"Lindsay, do you think your coin is close by?" Kirsty asked.

"I just don't know," Lindsay replied. "I

don't have a sense of where it is."

"Then let's keep looking," Rachel said.

The group was heading into the meadow now. Logan stopped by a stream. "This is Toby's Brook," he said. "It's named for Toberton's leprechaun. What a tricky little fellow! He's been helping the townspeople here for as long as anyone can remember."

"Did you hear that?" Lindsay whispered to her friends. "He said that the leprechaun *helps* people."

"Do you think he wants to help us?" Kirsty asked.

"Maybe," Rachel said. "We sure could use it."

"What is this?" Mr. Walker called out to Logan. He was pointing toward a very

large stone. It was as
tall as he was, and it
stood in the middle
of the brook.

"Oh, this is a
wishing stone," the
guide explained.
"Legend says that this
rock grants wishes. If
you can touch it without getting wet, your
wish will come true." Logan winked.

Kirsty looked at the stone. It was
placed at the widest part of the stream.

"I have a wish," a gruff voice called
out. "Let me touch it."

"Oh, no. It's a goblin," Rachel said
under her breath.

"Don't worry," Lindsay whispered.
"He won't get his wish."

The goblin stood on the edge of the
bank and reached for the stone. Kirsty
held her breath as he leaned closer,
closer . . . and then fell in! "Oh, it's cold,"
the goblin grumbled. "Help me out!"

"I knew he wouldn't get his wish,"
Lindsay said. "But guess what — I will!"
While everyone was looking at the soggy
goblin, the fairy flew to the stone.

Rachel and Kirsty crossed their fingers. When Lindsay touched the stone, there was a burst of sparkles. She smiled and quickly flew back to the girls.

"What happened?" Kirsty asked Lindsay.

"Did your wish come true?" said Rachel.

"We'll have to wait and see," Lindsay whispered. "I wished for a sign. A sign from Toby."

A Race to the Rainbow

Rachel and Kirsty jogged to catch up to the group. They looked around for a sign, but they didn't see anything special — until they looked up.

"Oh!" Rachel gasped. "What an amazing rainbow!"

"It looks like it leads all the way into town," Kirsty said.

"That's it!" Lindsay exclaimed from Rachel's shoulder. "That's the sign. We have to follow it."

"Lindsay, where will the rainbow take us?" Rachel asked.

"It should lead us straight to the gold coin," Lindsay said with a smile.

Too late, the girls realized that the goblins were right behind them.

"It's those pesky girls!" one of the goblins yelled. "And that fairy is with them!"

"I just heard them. The coin isn't here," cried a crooked-nosed goblin. "It's at the end of the rainbow!"

"We have to get it!" The group of goblins took off, running along the nature path.

Kirsty and Rachel looked at each other, worried. "We have to go!" Kirsty cried.

Rachel rushed up to her father and grabbed his hand. "Kirsty really wants to get back to town," she said. "She's excited about following that rainbow."

What she said was true — she just didn't mention the goblins, Lindsay, or the gold coin! "Oh," Mr. Walker responded. "Well, Logan just finished his talk. And

tracking a rainbow sounds like fun." He
let Rachel tug him toward their bikes.

"Hurry!" Kirsty said, clipping her
helmet on.

In no time, they were zooming down
the nature path.

Rachel asked her dad if she and Kirsty
could ride ahead, and the two girls
sped forward. They still hadn't spotted
the goblins.

"How will we catch up with them?" Kirsty asked nervously.

"Easily!" Lindsay replied. She flew off Rachel's shoulder and looked behind them. "The coast is clear," she called out. The fairy gave her wand a twirl, and a cloud of sparkles swirled around the bikes. The girls and the bikes began to shrink.

Then, the bikes began to lift into the air . . . with Rachel and Kirsty on them!

"We'll get there much faster if we fly!" Lindsay announced.

From high above, the girls could see the nature path and the tops of the trees. In the distance, they spotted the spire of the Toberton Town Hall.

"Look!" Kirsty cried. "We're right under the rainbow."

"And there's my dad," Rachel said, looking behind them.

"We're almost to Toberton," Lindsay said. The rainbow seemed to lead right to the town square. "We should land in the woods. It's safer."

The three friends flew lower in the sky. Just as they were dropping below the trees, Kirsty groaned. "Oh, no! The goblins are already here."

Lindsay changed Rachel and Kirsty back to their human size. When the three friends came out of the woods, the sun was behind the clouds. "We need the sun, so we can see where the rainbow leads," said Kirsty.

"It doesn't look like the festival will start on time," Rachel commented, looking around the town green. The game booths weren't up yet. The roof of the large party tent was sagging to the ground.

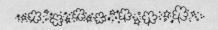

Lindsay peeked out from Kirsty's jacket
pocket.

Everywhere they looked, the
friends could see signs
that the lucky gold
coin was still
missing, but
they didn't
see the
goblins.
"What a
mess!"
Kirsty
said.
"Nothing
is going
as planned," complained
a man who was trying to hang a big

St. Patrick's Day banner. "I can't find
the right tools for the job."

"I wish we could help," Kirsty said.

"You can," Lindsay assured her. "We
just have to find the coin." As she said
it, the sun appeared from behind the
clouds and the rainbow shone in the
sky again.

"Quick, we have to find where it ends!" Rachel cried.

A Magical Wish

Looking up at the sky, Kirsty and
Rachel began to run. They followed
the colorful arch. And at the end of the
rainbow, they found . . .

"A wishing well!" Rachel cried. "It
must be a booth for the festival."

"Yup," said a man selling tickets. "Just
for today. Buy a lucky penny to throw

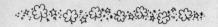

into the well. If you have the luck of the Irish, your wish will come true!"

The girls quickly dug in their pockets for some money. Together, they had just enough for one wish. But there were at least ten people in line before them! There were also people hanging around, watching. Some of them had on leprechaun costumes.

Oh, no — the goblins!

"We have to believe in the magic of the wishing well," Kirsty said.

"If we make the right wish, it will come true," Rachel agreed.

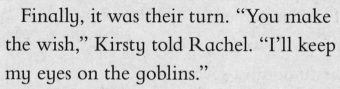

"My fingers are crossed, girls," said Lindsay from Kirsty's pocket.

Finally, it was their turn. "You make the wish," Kirsty told Rachel. "I'll keep my eyes on the goblins."

Rachel closed her eyes, made their wish, and threw the penny into the stone well. After a moment, she heard a splash.

All at once, a shiny gold coin zipped straight up out of the well. "Look!" Rachel cried.

"Get it!" yelled the goblins. A giant green hand reached out and hit the coin, flinging it higher into the air.

Kirsty stretched as high as she could, her arms smacking into lots of knobby green elbows. It was Kirsty against seven goblins! She held her breath as the gold coin began to fall back down. A long-fingered

goblin was about to snatch it when
Lindsay appeared!

The fairy flew right over all the grabby
hands and pulled the
gold coin into her arms.
Hooray! The coin
immediately shrunk
down to Fairyland size.
Lindsay blew a kiss to
the girls and disappeared
in a swirl of sparkles.

Kirsty and Rachel smiled
at each other. Whew!

The goblins ran off in a grumbly huff.
"It looks like things are finally going as
planned," Kirsty joked.

"Hello, girls," Mr. Walker called. He
waved as he rode up on his bike. "The

festival is looking good." He admired the game booths and the banner that now hung perfectly on the gazebo. The roof of the tent no longer sagged to the ground. "Your mom's speech is about to start. She can join us when she's done."

Rachel breathed a big sigh of relief.

"I'm going to take a quick look in the woods," Mr. Walker said. "I could have sworn I saw some pennywort when I rode by on my bike."

"That would be lucky," Rachel said with a laugh.

"Yes, it would," Mr. Walker agreed.

When he'd left, the girls went to a booth decorated with giant shamrocks to try a game. It was like a fishing game, but instead of fish in a pond, there were tiny green-suited leprechauns in boats. The boats bobbed in a stream that went through the green countryside.

"It looks like Toby's Brook," Rachel said. "There's even a big wishing rock by the woods."

A kind woman with red hair and freckles handed both girls fishing poles.

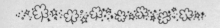

"Catch a leprechaun and you'll get a prize," she explained.

"These games are always harder than they look," Kirsty said, trying to balance her pole over the moving leprechauns.

"And it's almost impossible to catch a real leprechaun," Rachel added. She placed her pole over one of the tiny boats. Then, as if by magic, there were leprechauns hanging from the ends of both poles at the same time!

"Wow, you must be the luckiest girls at the festival!" the woman exclaimed. "I have the perfect prize for the two of you." She handed each girl a shamrock-shaped case. What could be inside?

"Thank you," Rachel and Kirsty said and waved good-bye.

They went
over to a
bench and
sat down so
that they
could open
their prizes.
"Oh, it's
beautiful!"

Rachel said, lifting a bracelet in the air.
The bracelet had several charms hanging
from it: a bowler hat, a shamrock, a gold
coin, a rainbow, and a leprechaun.

"There's a note," Kirsty added. *"I wish
you all the luck in the world — Lindsay."*

Rachel looked more closely at the
charms. "I wonder if this leprechaun charm
is Toby."

"I wonder if Toby is watching us right now," Kirsty said.

Rachel giggled. "I think that Toby the Toberton leprechaun is as clever as they come," Rachel admitted. "We might not ever know the truth about him."

"Yes, but I know that we were very lucky to have his help," Kirsty added with a wink.

"We really are the luckiest girls at the festival," Rachel said. "We're lucky to have the fairies — and each other — as true friends!"

SPECIAL EDITION

Don't miss any of Rachel and Kirsty's
other fairy adventures!
Check out this magical sneak peek of

Brianna
the Tooth Fairy!

Tooth
Trouble

Rachel Walker opened her bedroom
window and leaned out to gaze up at the
starry sky. She took a deep breath of
fresh air and smiled happily.

"This is going to be the best summer
ever," she said.

Her best friend, Kirsty Tate, had
arrived that morning to stay with her in

Tippington. Three long, sunny weeks stretched ahead of them. Rachel couldn't wait to find out what adventures awaited them. Whenever they were together, the most exciting and magical things seemed to happen!

She heard her bedroom door open and turned around. Kirsty came in, carrying something small in the palm of her hand.

"Rachel, guess what?" she said. "My loose tooth has finally fallen out!"

"That's terrific!" said Rachel. "We can put it under your pillow, so the Tooth Fairy can come tonight."

She closed the curtains and both girls changed into their pajamas. Then Kirsty slid her tooth under her pillow and patted it down happily.

"We've never met the Tooth Fairy, have we?" she asked, climbing under the covers. "I wonder what she's like."

Rachel and Kirsty had a very special secret. They were friends with lots of fairies and had visited Fairyland many times. Sometimes Jack Frost made trouble with his goblins. The girls had often helped the fairies foil his plans.

"Maybe we'll wake up when she comes to exchange your tooth for money," said Rachel. She got into bed and yawned.

"The Tooth Fairy is so quiet that she never wakes anyone up," said Kirsty.

Rachel smiled and turned out her bedside light. It had been a long day, and within a few minutes, both girls were fast asleep.

When Rachel's alarm went off in the morning, she sat up and looked eagerly over to where her best friend was sleeping.

"Kirsty, wake up!" she said. "Let's see what the Tooth Fairy brought you!"

Kirsty sat up and lifted her pillow. Then her shoulders slumped.

"My tooth is still here," she said, disappointed.

Rachel jumped out of bed and came over to sit with Kirsty. Sure enough, the little white tooth was still lying on the sheet.

"The Tooth Fairy is probably confused because you're staying here instead of at your house," she said, putting her arm around Kirsty. "I'm sure she'll come tonight."

"Maybe she left some money but forgot to take the tooth," said Kirsty. She picked up the pillow and shook it. "Or maybe the money got stuck inside the pillowcase?"

As she shook the pillow, the girls heard a faint tinkling noise. Suddenly, a tiny fairy came shooting out of the pillowcase. She did three somersaults in the air and landed on Kirsty's nightstand. She was wearing a ruffled skirt with funky red boots and a polka-dotted top. Her long golden hair curled over her shoulder.

"Hello, Kirsty and Rachel!" she said. "I'm Brianna the Tooth Fairy." She smiled.

"Hi, Brianna," said Rachel. "Are you here to take Kirsty's tooth?"

"I wish I was," said Brianna, looking upset. "But Jack Frost has been causing trouble again. I've come to ask for your help."

"What happened?" asked Kirsty.

"I'll show you," said Brianna. She waved her wand at the mirror hanging on the wall, and the surface rippled. When it was smooth again, Rachel's bedroom had disappeared. Instead, the girls saw Jack Frost's scowling face in the reflection!

Jack Frost was sitting on his throne with a hand clamped to the side of his face. He moaned and groaned at the top of his voice. Goblins scurried around his feet, cringing as he shouted.

"None of your silly cures work!" he roared. "I've tried rubbing garlic, potatoes, ice cubes, and pepper onto my gums, and nothing works! My tooth still hurts!"

He kicked a tray that a warty-nosed goblin was holding. A toothbrush, some floss, and a tube of toothpaste flew through the air. The goblin dropped to his hands and knees to pick them up.

"Maybe you should go see the dentist," muttered the goblin.

The whole throne room went deadly silent. Jack Frost sat up very straight. The other goblins backed away.

"*What* did you say?" hissed Jack Frost.

The warty-nosed goblin looked around and realized that he was on his own. His bottom lip started to tremble.

"N-nothing," he babbled, scooping everything onto his tray and crawling out of Jack Frost's reach.

"I never want to hear the word 'dentist' in this room again!" screeched Jack Frost.

"But how are you going to get rid of your toothache without a den . . . um . . . without help?" asked the goblin.

Jack Frost snarled and banged his fist down on the arm of his throne. "If only I had the Tooth Fairy's magic — I bet my teeth would be perfect!"

RAINBOW magic

These activities are magical!
Play dress-up, send friendship notes, and much more!

RAINBOW magic™

There's Magic in Every Series!

The Rainbow Fairies
The Weather Fairies
The Jewel Fairies
The Pet Fairies
The Fun Day Fairies
The Petal Fairies
The Dance Fairies
The Music Fairies
The Sports Fairies
The Party Fairies
The Ocean Fairies
The Night Fairies
The Magical Animal Fairies
The Princess Fairies
The Superstar Fairies

Read them all!

▮ SCHOLASTIC

scholastic.com
rainbowmagiconline.com

HiT entertainment

RMFAIRY7